Watch Me Swim

written by Pam Holden
illustrated by Christine Hansen

1

"I can swim fast,"
said the frog.

"I can swim fast,"
said the turtle.

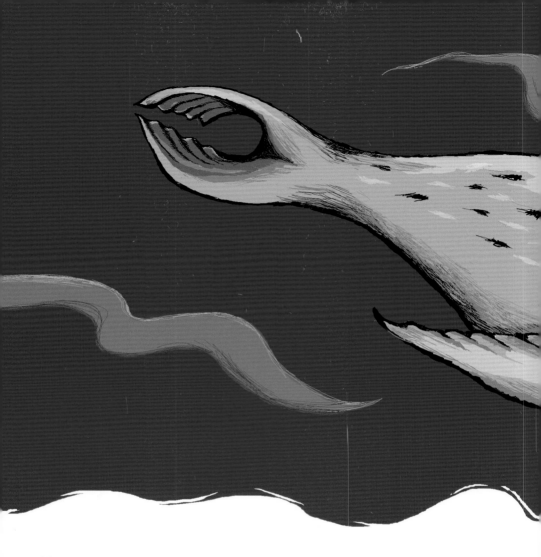

"I can swim fast,"
said the seal.

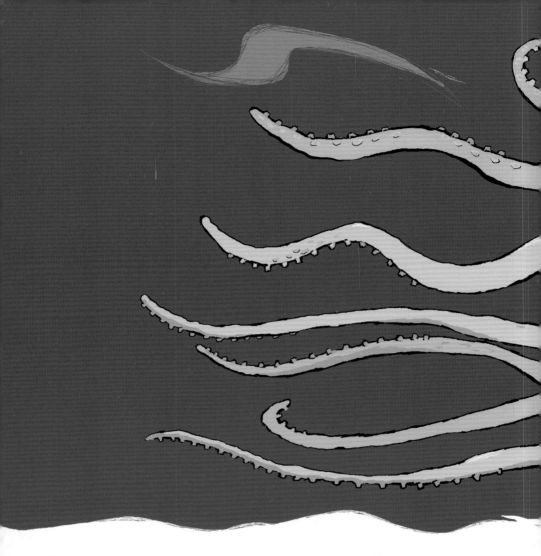

"I can swim fast,"
said the octopus.

"I can swim fast," said the whale.

"I can swim fast,"
said the shark.

"I can swim fast,"
said the fish.

"I can swim fast too," said the penguin.